Sweet Clara AND THE Freedom Quilt

by DEBORAH HOPKINSON
paintings by JAMES RANSOME

Alfred A. Knopf : New York

THIS IS A BORZOI BOOK
PUBLISHED BY ALFRED A. KNOPF, INC.

Manufactured in the United States of America
Book design by Mina Greenstein   4   5   6   7   8   9   10

Library of Congress Cataloging-in-Publication Data
Hopkinson, Deborah.
Sweet Clara and the freedom quilt / by Deborah Hopkinson ;
illustrated by James Ransome.   p.   cm.
Summary: A young slave stitches a quilt with a map pattern which guides her to
freedom in the North.
ISBN 0-679-82311-5 (trade) — ISBN 0-679-92311-X (lib. bdg.)
[1. Slavery—Fiction. 2. Quilts—Fiction.]   I. Title.   PZ7.H778125Sw   1993
[E]—dc20   91-11601

For my father and in memory of my mother
—D. H.

For Emma Ransom, the first slave of
Pattie and General Matt W. Ransom, and all the other
Ransom slaves on Verona Plantation
—J. R.

$\mathcal{B}$EFORE I WAS EVEN TWELVE YEARS OLD, I got sent from North Farm to Home Plantation 'cause they needed another field hand. When I got there, I cried so much they thought I was never gon' eat or drink again. I didn't want to leave my momma.

"I'm goin' back to her," I whispered every day to Young Jack, who worked beside me in the fields.

"Well, you better start eatin' all you can, Sweet Clara." He smiled at me. But then his smile was gone. In a low voice he say, "Or else you won't make it."

Young Jack helped me believe I'd get back to my momma someday. Truth was, I'd be lost before I got through the fields, them being so big and all. But I didn't give up dreamin'.

Aunt Rachel was raising me now. She wasn't my for-real blood aunt, but she did her best to care for me.

One night she come back from working in the Big House and found me lying dead tired on our cabin floor. She shook her head and say, "Sweet Clara, you aine gon' last in the fields. But I got an idea."

Aunt Rachel's idea was sewin'—and she started teachin' me the very next night. It wasn't easy for me to learn, my hands already rough and clumsy from hoeing and weeding the fields. So Aunt Rachel took it real slow.

She brought scraps of cloth from the Big House and taught me 'bout each one, how it was special and had to be treated in its own way. I liked to piece the scraps together to make pretty patterns of colors. But Aunt Rachel didn't care much about pretty patterns.

"Now you rip out that whole row and do it again, Clara," she say.

"Why I got to make the stitches so tiny?" I complained.

"You gon' be a real *seamstress*, that's why."

"Tomorrow you comin' with me to the Big House. I got it all worked out," Aunt Rachel say one day.

I was frightened.

"You ready to sew with me," she went on. "Missus' daughter Ella be gettin' married come spring. I told Missus I'd be needin' help. She look at yo' work with sharp eyes, Clara, so do it quick and neat like I taught you."

Next morning I tried to eat some corn bread, but my insides was all knotted up. I never been inside the Big House before or seen white people that close — 'cept the overseer.

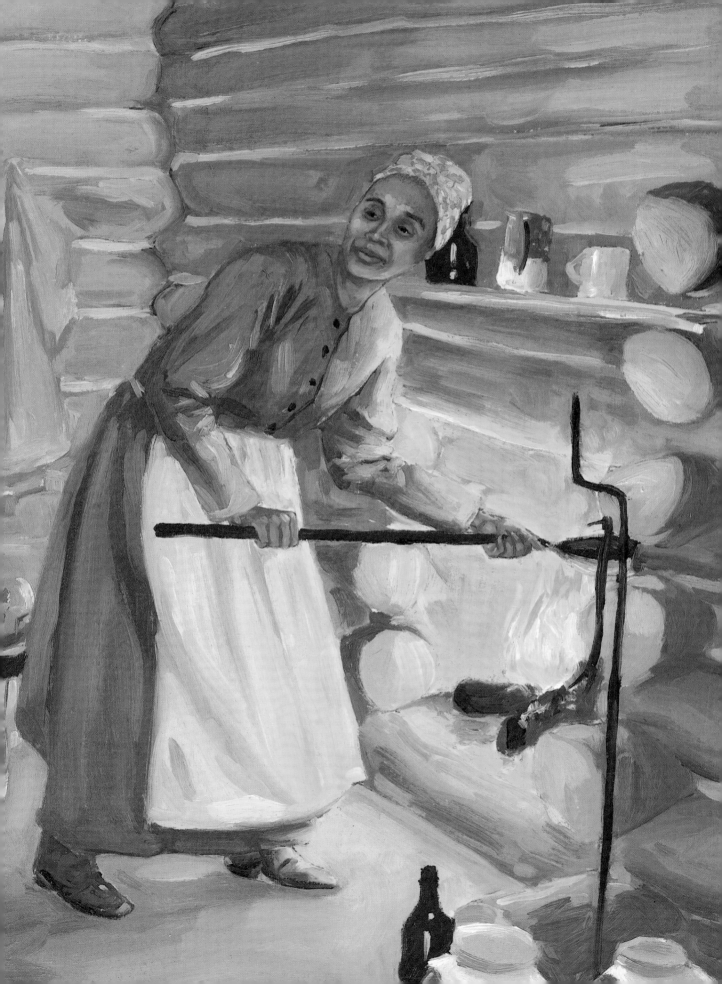

The morning sun was streamin' into the sewin' room, turning everything all sunflower yellow. Aunt Rachel give me some sheets to hem. Instead of being contrary, that needle did all I wanted, just like it was part of my hand.

At the end of the day, Missus come in. "Let me see your work, Clara," she say.

I gave her the sheet, and she ran it through her hands real slow. I held my breath, watching.

"From now on, come here," she say at last.

When she left, Aunt Rachel and I looked at each other, about ready to burst. "We done it, girl!" she cried.

So I changed from a field hand to a seamstress. Since the sewin' room was right off the kitchen, Aunt Rachel and I were near Cook and the helpers. There was always lots of bustle and company in the kitchen. I was hearing about all kinds of new places and things. I listened so hard it felt like my ears must be growing right out of my head and gettin' big with listening.

One day two white men come to see the master. The drivers went into the kitchen to talk to Cook.

"There been too many runaways last summer," one of the drivers said. "They goin' round askin' all the masters in the county to join the paterollers."

"Crazy, runnin' away," muttered Cook as she beat up some batter. "Where you gon' get to 'cept lost in the swamp?"

"Dunno," said the other. "But I hear we aine that far from the Ohio River. Once you get that far, the Underground Railroad will carry you across."

"That's right," agreed the first. "The Railroad will get you all the way to Canada. Then you free forever."

Cook snorted. "If it be as easy as you two let on, more woulda gone."

One of the men replied in a quiet voice, "It be easy if you could get a map."

Walking back from the Big House that evening I asked Aunt Rachel 'bout what I'd heard. "Where's Canada? And what's the Underground Railroad?"

"See there?" Aunt Rachel pointed. "That's the North Star. Under that star, far up north, is Canada. The Underground Railroad is people who been helpin' folks get there, secret-like."

She looked at me hard. "But don't you start thinkin' 'bout it. You run away and get caught, you be beaten."

Still, I couldn't *stop* thinking about it. Next day I asked Cook, "Those two men that was here yesterday. They was talking 'bout a map. What's a map?"

"Just a picture of the land, that's all. Whatever's on the ground, a map can have it."

Sunday I went to my favorite place on the little hill and looked out at the people's cabins and the fields. I took a stick and started making a picture in the dirt of all I could see.

But how could I make a picture of things far away that I *couldn't* see? And how could I make a map that wouldn't be washed away by the rain — a map that would show the way to freedom?

Then one day I was sewin' a patch on a pretty blue blanket. The patch looked just the same shape as the cow pond near the cabins. The little stitches looked like a path going all round it. Here it was — a picture that wouldn't wash away. A map!

So I started the quilt.

When you sewin', no matter how careful you be, little scraps of cloth always be left after you cut out a dress or a pillowcase. So while my ears kept listening, and my hands kept sewin', I began to squirrel away these bits of cloth.

When we was off work, I went to visit people in the Quarters. I started askin' what fields was where. Then I started piecin' the scraps of cloth with the scraps of things I was learnin'.

Aunt Rachel say, "Sweet Clara, what kind of pattern you makin' in that quilt? Aine no pattern I ever seen."

"I don't know, Aunt Rachel. I'm just patchin' it together as I go." She looked at me long, but she just nodded.

There was a buzzing in the Quarters one summer evening. I saw the paterollers and I knew someone had run away. It was Young Jack. But five days later they caught him.

That next Sunday I went to see him, and we walked to the top of the little hill. He didn't smile the way he used to.

I took a stick and began to draw in the dirt. I drew a little square for Big House, a line of boxes for the cabins of the Quarters, and some bigger squares for the fields east of Big House. I drew as much as I'd pieced together.

Jack sat beside me, not sayin' anything. Not even looking at first. Then he started seeing what I was doing. I handed the stick to him. I hear him catch his breath up quick. Then he begun to draw.

I worked on the quilt for a long time. Sometimes months would go by and I wouldn't get any pieces sewn in it. Sometimes I had to wait to get the right kind of cloth — I had blue calico and flowered blue silk for creeks and rivers, and greens and blue-greens for the fields, and white sheeting for roads. Missus liked to wear pink a lot, so Big House, the Quarters, and finally, the Big House at North Farm, they was all pink.

The quilt got bigger and bigger, and if folks knew what I was doin', no one said. But they came by the sewin' room to pass the time of day whenever they could.

"By the way, Clara," a driver might tell me, "I heard the master sayin' yesterday he didn't want to travel to Mr. Morse's place 'cause it's over twenty miles north o' here."

Or someone would sit eatin' Cook's food and say, so as I could hear, "Word is they gon' plant corn in the three west fields on the Verona plantation this year."

When the master went out huntin', Cook's husband was the guide. He come back and say, "That swamp next to Home Plantation is a nasty place. But listen up, Clara, and I'll tell you how I thread my way in and out of there as smooth as yo' needle in that cloth."

Then one night the quilt was done. I looked at it spread out in the dim light of the cabin. Aunt Rachel studied it for the longest time. She touched the stitches lightly, her fingers moving slowly over the last piece I'd added—a hidden boat that would carry us across the Ohio River. Finally, they came to rest on the bright star at the top.

She tried to make her voice cheery. "You always did like to make patterns and pictures, Clara. You get yourself married to Young Jack one of these days, and you two will have a real nice quilt to sleep under."

"Aunt Rachel, I couldn't sleep under this quilt," I answered softly, putting my hand over hers. "Wouldn't be restful, somehow. Anyway, I think it should stay here. Maybe others can use it."

Aunt Rachel sighed. "But aine you gon' need the quilt where you goin'?"

I kissed her. "Don't worry, Aunt Rachel. I got the memory of it in my head."

It rained hard for three days the next week. Me and Jack left Home Plantation in a dark thunderstorm. The day after, it was too stormy to work in the fields, so Jack wasn't missed. And Aunt Rachel told them I was sick.

We went north, following the trail of the freedom quilt. All the things people told me about, all the tiny stitches I took, now I could see real things. There was the old tree struck down by lightning, the winding road near the creek, the hunting path through the swamp. It was like being in a dream you already dreamed.

Mostly we hid during the day and walked at night. When we got to North Farm, Jack slipped in through the darkness to find what cabin my momma at. Then we went in to get her and found a little sister I didn't even know I had. Momma was so surprised.

"Sweet Clara! You growed so big!" Her eyes just like I remembered, her arms strong around me.

"Momma, I'm here for you. We goin' North. We know the way."

I was afraid they wouldn't come. But then Momma say yes. Young Jack carried my sister Anna, and I held on to Momma's hand.

We kept on as fast as we could, skirting farms and towns and making our way through the woods. At last, one clear dark night, we come to the Ohio River. The river was high, but I remembered the place on the quilt where I'd marked the crossing. We searched the brush along the banks until at last we found the little boat.

"This was hid here by the folks in the Underground Railroad," I said.

The boat carried us across the dark, deep water to the other side. Shivering and hungry and scared, we stood looking ahead.

"Which way now?" Jack asked me.

I pointed. The North Star was shining clear above us. "Up there through the woods. North. To Canada."

SOMETIMES I THINK BACK TO THE NIGHT WE LEFT, when Young Jack come to wake me. I can still see Aunt Rachel sitting up in her bed. She just shook her head before I could say a word.

"Before you go, just cover me with your quilt, Sweet Clara," she say. "I'm too old to walk, but not too old to dream. And maybe I can help others follow the quilt to freedom."

Aunt Rachel kept her word. The quilt is there still, at Home Plantation. People go look at it, even folks from neighboring farms. I know because some of them come and tell me how they used it to get free. But not all are as lucky as we were, and most never can come.

Sometimes I wish I could sew a quilt that would spread over the whole land, and the people just follow the stitches to freedom, as easy as taking a Sunday walk.

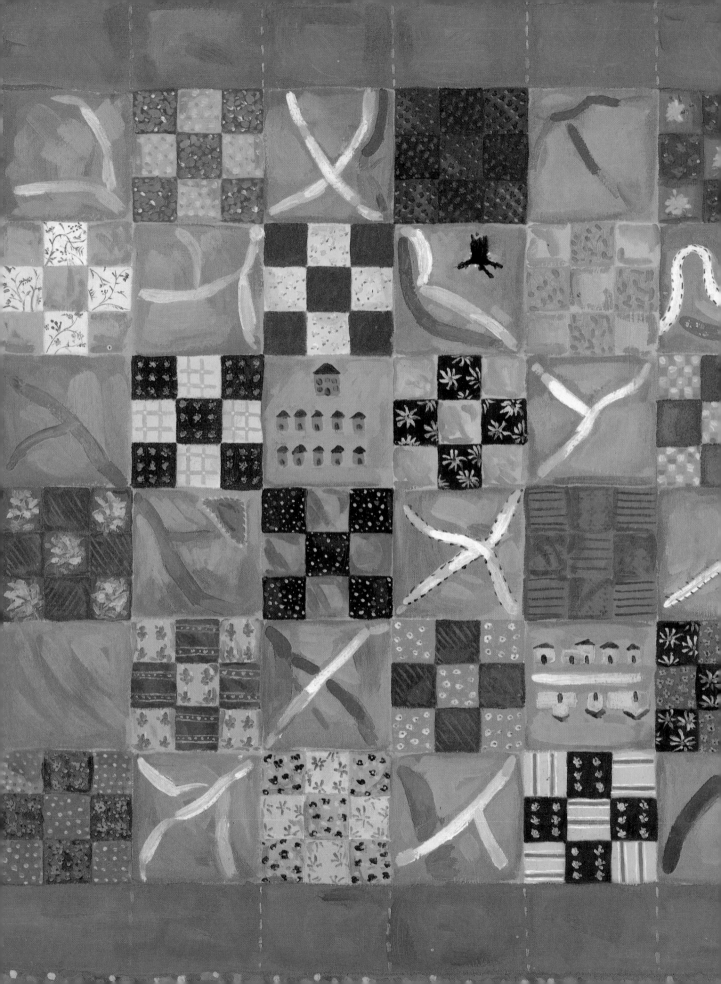